CONTENTS

...than Lueth

raintree

Raintree is an imprint of Capstone Global Library Limited, a company incorporated
in England and Wales having its registered office at 264 Banbury Road, Oxford, OX2
7DY – Registered company number: 6695582

www.raintree.co.uk
myorders@raintree.co.uk

Art Director: Heather Kindseth
Graphic Designer: Brann Garvey
Production Specialist: Kathy McCc
Original illustrations © 2009
Illustrated by Nathan Lueth
Originated by Capstone Global Lib
Printed and bound in India

ISBN 978 1 4747 7156 6
22 21 20 19 18
10 9 8 7 6 5 4 3 2 1

British Library Cataloguing in Publication Data
A full catalogue record for this book is available from the British Library.

Chapter 1

DAD'S SURPRISE

Connor Lander's dad was up to something. He'd been saying weird things for weeks. He kept dropping hints that the family was going to go somewhere. So when Connor walked into the living room, he didn't think twice about the big smile on his dad's face.

"It's going to be so great," Connor's dad said. "You guys are going to have a blast!"

"I'm sure we will," Connor replied. "So, what are we going to do?"

"You'll see," Dad said, giving Connor a wink.

Shayla, Connor's sister, came out of her room and sat down on the sofa. "Is Dad still talking about the surprise?" she asked.

"Yep," Connor replied. "Just like every day."

"I bet it's an amazing holiday," Shayla said. "Or we're buying a new car."

Dad just smiled again and said, "You'll see."

Connor wandered into the kitchen. His mum was unpacking the shopping. Connor started to help her.

"Mum," Connor asked, "what's the big secret? Dad makes it sound like it'll be the best thing ever."

"You know what your dad's like," said Mum. "He likes things to be a surprise. He'd be upset if I told you."

Shayla walked in. She began to help Mum unpack the bags.

"Can't you give us a hint?" Shayla asked.

Mum smiled. "Let's just say it'll build character," she told them.

Connor and Shayla looked at each other nervously. If their mum said something would build character, it was not going to be any fun.

Dad walked into the kitchen. He was wearing his winter coat and a thick, warm hat. "It's time for us to get going," he said. "Get dressed, everyone. You'll need to stay warm."

Connor put on a heavy jumper. Then he pulled on his winter coat, scarf and hat.

Everyone piled into the car. Dad drove to a part of town Connor had never seen before. There were new houses being built. Almost all of them were unfinished. Dad parked the car in front of a house that looked like it was nearly finished.

"Where are we?" Connor asked.

"This is our family project," said Dad. "We're going to build a house!"

Chapter 2

BUILD A WHAT?

"We're going to build a what?" asked Connor.

"Your father is exaggerating," said Mum. "We're not building the house. It's mostly built already. We're going to help finish building this house."

Dad opened the car door and stepped out into the cold winter air. He clapped his hands together. "Let's go!" he said.

Connor and Shayla followed their parents into the house. Inside there were lots of people working. Some were putting up walls, some were on ladders installing lights and some were pounding or drilling. It was so cold in the house that Connor could see his own breath.

A woman with long brown hair and a hard hat came over to them. "Welcome to Habitat for Humanity," she said, smiling. "You must be the Lander family. I'm so glad you're here to help. My name is Reba. I'm the leader of this job."

"What's Habitat for Humanity?" asked Shayla. "Is it like that makeover programme on TV?"

Reba smiled. "Sort of," she said. "It's an organization that builds homes for people who need them. We ask for volunteers like you to help us build the houses."

"That's why we're here," said Dad. "To help put the finishing touches on this house."

"Cool!" said Connor. "Will I get to use power tools or something?"

Reba laughed. "Not quite," she said. "Let's get started. Here are some helmets and safety glasses for all of you. Mrs Lander and Shayla, you can join Mr Givens outside to help with the deck. Mr Lander, would you mind cutting and laying the tiles in the bathroom?"

"No problem!" Dad said.

"What will I get to do?" asked Connor. "Smash a wall with a sledgehammer? Nail some two by fours with a nail gun?"

"Actually, we were hoping you would paint one of the bedrooms," Reba said, handing him a paintbrush.

Connor groaned. He said, "Painting sounds boring and stupid. I want to use power tools!"

"Connor, all of the jobs we're doing are important," Mum said.

Shayla stuck her tongue out. Then she said, "Yeah, Connor! Now go to your room!"

Chapter 3

#

Reba led Connor down the corridor to a bedroom. Two tins of paint sat on the floor. The paint was white. There wasn't a more boring colour in the whole world. Connor knew he was going to hate his job.

"Make sure you get the paint all the way up to the ceiling," Reba said. "There's a ladder just outside the door if you need to use one."

Reba left. Connor looked around the room. The floors were still unfinished, but the room looked pretty big. Connor thought that he wouldn't mind having the room himself. It seemed like a nice room.

He started painting on the left side of the room. At first, he made a lot of mistakes. He didn't stir the paint and it went on too thick. Then it was too thin. Then he spilled some on the floor.

After a while, Connor started to enjoy himself. He just turned up his MP3 player and painted.

An hour later, he stepped back to see how his paint job looked. He had only painted half of one of the walls.

It was going to take forever to finish the whole room!

Just then, Reba came back into the room. A boy who looked like he was Connor's age walked in behind her.

"It looks great in here, Connor!" Reba said. "I have some help for you. This is Max."

"Hi, Max," said Connor.

"Hey," Max replied. He just kept staring at the ground.

Great, Connor thought. The job was boring, the paint was boring and now his helper was boring, too.

"I'll leave you to get to work," Reba said as she looked around the room. "You have a lot to do."

After she left, Connor handed Max a paintbrush.

"Here you go," Connor said.

"Whatever," said Max.

Connor knew it was going to be a long day.

Chapter 4

They painted in silence for twenty minutes. Finally, Connor couldn't take it anymore. He decided to try to talk to Max.

"So, where do you go to school?" Connor asked. "I haven't seen you at Armstrong Middle School."

Max didn't even look up from his paintbrush. "I don't go there," he said.

"Oh," said Connor. Another silent minute went by. "So where do you go?" Connor asked.

Max sighed. Then he said, "I go to Lincoln Middle School. It's down the street from here."

Connor could tell that Max didn't want to talk. He didn't ask any more questions.

Soon, Connor finished his wall. He needed to move to the next wall. He picked up the paintbrush and a paint tin. Then he walked to the other side of the room.

As he was putting the tin of paint down, it slipped from his hands and hit the floor. Paint splashed out of the tin and hit him in the face.

Max laughed.

"That wasn't funny," said Connor, wiping paint off his nose.

"Yeah it was," Max said.

Connor flicked some paint at Max. A white blob of paint exploded on Max's shoulder.

"Hey!" said Max.

"I suppose you're right," Connor said, smiling. "It is pretty funny."

Connor flicked a little more paint at Max. Max ducked and flung some back at Connor. Some of the paint hit Connor on the leg, but the rest landed on the wall behind him.

Connor reached into the tin and scooped up paint. Then he ran at Max.

"Here it comes!" Connor yelled.

Max tried to get out of the way, but he couldn't. Connor wiped paint in Max's hair. Max laughed. Then he ran his paintbrush across Connor's face.

Connor dumped the entire contents of the paint tin over Max. At the same time, Max dumped his tin over Connor.

Just then, Reba flung the door open. "What is going on in here?" she yelled.

Chapter 5

Reba looked shocked. "What have you two been doing?" she asked. She looked around the paint-covered room.

"It was all my fault," Max said, trying not to laugh. "I hit Connor with some paint and he threw some back."

"This room is a mess," said Reba. "We need you two to help finish this house, not tear it apart! Now clean up this mess and finish this paint job!"

Reba left the room. She shut the door loudly behind her.

When they were sure it was safe, both boys looked at each other. Then they burst out laughing.

"Wow, she was really angry," said Max. "She looked like her head was going to explode!"

"I know," said Connor. "I thought that look she gave us would take the paint off the walls by itself. But why did you take the blame? I was the one who hit you first with the paint."

Max shrugged. He said, "I thought Reba wouldn't get angry at me."

"Why not?" Connor asked, frowning.

"Because it's my house," Max said.

"What? I thought it was going to a poor family," said Connor.

Max looked at the ground. Then he said, "My dad lost his job last year and my mum is too ill to work. We moved into a shelter for a couple of months. Then Habitat for Humanity offered to help us with this house."

Max and Connor were quiet for a while. Then Max said, "It's really cool that people like you will volunteer to help out people who need it."

"I almost didn't want to come here today," said Connor. "I thought it was going to be boring and stupid. But painting is actually fun. And it was cool to meet you."

Max smiled. Then he looked around at the mess. "I suppose we should start cleaning up my room," he said.

"This is your room?" Connor asked. "Now I do feel bad about the mess."

"Don't worry about it," said Max. "Every time I look at the walls, I'll remember what a great time we had today."

Max and Connor cleaned up the floor and re-painted the walls. By the time they finished, it was impossible to tell they had made such a mess.

In one corner of the room, they lifted the plastic sheet off the floor. Then they each dipped a hand in the leftover paint and made a handprint on the wooden floor.

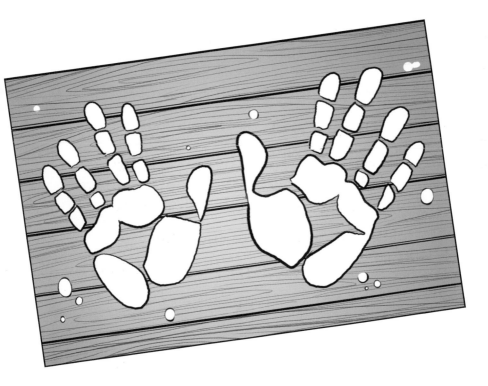

"It's sort of like how a painter signs his name on his paintings," Connor said.

"Cool!" Max said.

They went out to the front of the house to join the rest of the volunteers.

"Where are you staying until your house is finished?" asked Connor.

"We're just staying a few more nights at the shelter," Max told him.

Connor thought for a minute. Then he said, "Maybe you could stay with us for a day or so. I think my room could use a new coat of paint. And we already proved we're the best painters in town!"

ABOUT THE AUTHOR

Jon Mikkelsen has written several plays for kids, which have involved aliens, superheroes and more aliens. He acts on stage and loves performing in front of an audience. Jon also loves sushi, cheeseburgers and pizza. He loves to travel, and has visited Moscow, Berlin, London and Amsterdam. He lives in Minnesota, USA, and has a cat called Coco, who does not pay rent.

ABOUT THE ILLUSTRATOR

Nathan Lueth has been a freelance illustrator since 2004. He graduated from the Minneapolis College of Art and Design in 2004, and has done work for companies such as Target, General Mills and Wreked Records. Nathan was a 2008 finalist in Tokyopop's Rising Stars of Manga contest. He lives in Minneapolis, Minnesota, USA.

GLOSSARY

blame say something is someone else's fault

character if something builds character, it makes you a better person

exaggerating making something seem bigger, better or more important than it is

hints clues or helpful tips

impossible if something is impossible, it is unable to be done or cannot be true

installing putting something in place, ready to be used

organization number of people working together

project something being worked on

shelter place where a homeless person can stay

unfinished not finished

DISCUSSION QUESTIONS

1. Do you think Connor's dad's surprise was good or bad? Why?

2. Why do you think Max didn't talk much when he first met Connor?

3. Do you think it would be fun to help build a house? What part of building a house would you want to help with?

WRITING PROMPTS

1. What would your dream house be like? Describe it. Then draw a picture of your house and label the rooms.

2. Sometimes it can be interesting to think about a story from another person's point of view. Try writing chapter 4 from Max's point of view. What does he see and hear? What does he think about? How does he feel?

3. What do you think happens after this book ends? Write about what Max and Connor do after they've finished painting Max's room.

FIND OUT MORE

Want to find out more about some of the topics covered in this book? Here are some fiction and non-fiction books to get you started, as well as some websites that may be useful.

Fiction

The Double Life of Zoe Flynn, Janet Lee Carey (Atheneum Books, 2004)

Invisible Girl, Kate Maryon (Harper Collins Children's Books, 2013)

Katie and the Ducklings (City Farm), Jessie Williams (Curious Fox, 2013)

Non-fiction

Coping with Unemployment (Real Life Issues), Mary Colson (Raintree, 2012)

The Hidden Story of Homelessness (Undercover Story), Karen Latchana Kenney (Raintree, 2016)

Poverty (Our World in Crisis), Rachel Minay (Franklin Watts, 2018)

www.childline.org.uk

Childline is a charity and support system for children of all ages. You can talk to Childline counsellors about anything: homelessness, bullying, your family, your school life.

england.shelter.org.uk

Shelter is a charity that helps and advises homeless people in the UK.

www.habitatforhumanity.org.uk

Habitat For Humanity International is a non-profit organization that works to wipe out poverty and homelessness around the world.

www.savethechildren.org.uk/what-we-do/child-poverty

Learn more about what the charity Save the Children does to help children in poverty.

IF YOU LIKE THIS BOOK CHECK OUT...

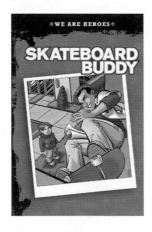